This

PLAYDATE KIDS

Book

belongs to:

_____

Chloe   Cosmos   Danny   Dakota

For my grandchildren Brian, Mary, Matthew, Seth, Owen and Clara
and to all the children I've helped for the past 34 years in Malibu, my hometown - A.T.

For Julian - W.M.E.

Chloe's New Baby Brother

by
Annie Thiel, Ph.D.

illustrated by
Karen Marjoribanks
&
William M. Edwards

PLAYDATE KIDS PUBLISHING
LOS ANGELES

A TENA FANNING
PUBLICATION

Chloe was very excited.

"Today my new baby brother, David, is coming home!" she told her dog, Scootch. Chloe didn't have any brothers or sisters, so she didn't know what to expect. But she did know one thing.

"I'm going to be his big sister," she said, "and that's an important job."

Chloe and Dad had visited Mom and David at the hospital. "We have to stay here for a few more days so the doctors can make sure David is healthy," Mom had said.

Finally, Mom and Dad brought David home.
"Welcome home, David!" Chloe cheered.
"I'm your big sister, Chloe!"

Chloe showed David all the pretty pictures she had drawn to welcome him to the family.

"Look, David, these are for you!" she told him.

"Why doesn't he like me?" Chloe asked.
David's loud crying scared her.

Dad explained to Chloe that babies cry a lot.
He said, "When babies cry, it usually means
that they're hungry or tired."

"You cried a lot when you were a baby, too," Mom added.

"Babies do not know how to talk
or ask questions," Dad explained,
"not like big kids."

"Big kids can also ask questions when they don't understand something," Dad told her. "Babies have to cry to tell us something is wrong."

The next day, Chloe learned that Mom and Dad had to spend lots of time taking care of David.

They had to feed him...

...change his diapers...

...rock him when he cried...

...and play with him.

Chloe used her words and told her parents how she was feeling. "Sometimes I love having a new baby brother," she said, "but sometimes I feel left out."

"Babies need lots of attention," Mom told her. "David needs it now, just like you did when you were a baby."

Chloe shared her feelings about David with her grandmother.
"Sometimes I wish I was the baby," Chloe said.

"It's okay to feel that way," Grandma told her. "But, remember that even though babies get a lot of attention, there are many fun things that are only for big kids."

...and played board games together after David went to sleep at night.

One night, they even had pizza and ice cream for dinner!

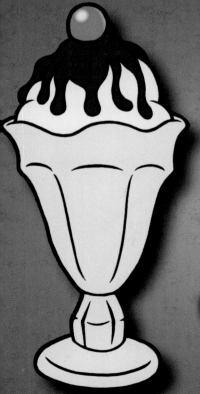

David couldn't eat these special treats. "It's only for big kids," Mom said.

YUMMY CHOKLIT

"Because you're David's big sister,
we might need your help sometimes," Dad said.

"I don't mind," said Chloe.

Sometimes, Mom had Chloe hold her baby brother in her rocking chair.

"Be gentle, Chloe," Mom told her. "Babies are very delicate and need special care."

Sometimes, Chloe sang special songs to David and showed him how to play with her favorite toys.

But Chloe's favorite thing was to make funny faces at David to make him laugh.

Chloe knew that being a big sister meant sharing
her parents with her new baby brother.
But she also knew that she had a great new friend to
play with and help take care of.

"Remember no one else can be David's big sister," Dad told her.
"I know," Chloe said. "Anyone can be a baby,
but it takes a big kid to be a big sister."

Things to Remember When a Baby Comes Home

1. You will probably have lots of different feelings when the new baby comes home. This is okay.

2. Talk to someone you trust about your feelings.

3. Don't be afraid to ask questions.

4. You are very special and no one can ever take your place in your family.

5. You can draw a picture to welcome home your new baby brother or sister.

6. Big kids can do a lot of fun things that babies cannot.

7. Just because the baby needs a lot of attention does not mean that your mom and dad have forgotten about you.

8. When you were a small baby, your mom and dad gave you lots of attention, too.

9. Ask your parents lots of questions about how to help take care of your new baby.

10. Being a big brother or sister is an important job.
    It can be fun to teach your new brother or sister how to do things

Draw a picture of your new baby brother or sister.

MORE THE PLAYDATE KIDS BOOKS

LET'S BE FRIENDS!

Danny O'Brien

The O'Briens move to a new town.

Cosmos McCool

Cosmos' parents get a divorce.

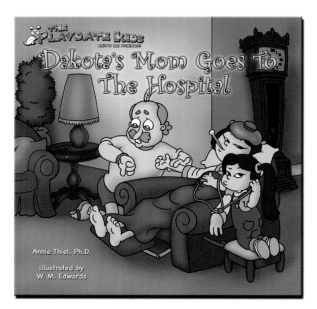

Dakota Greenblatt

Dakota's mom goes to the hospital.

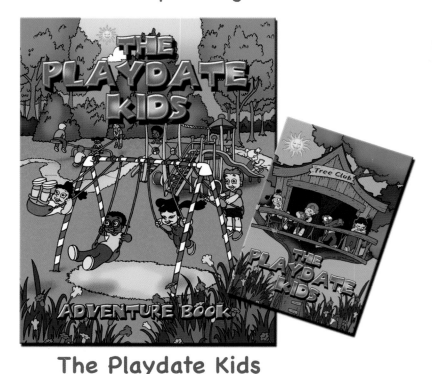

The Playdate Kids

Behavioral themed
coloring and puzzle book
AND animated cartoon DVD set!